POLLIWOG

To Ethan !
Best Wishes
Tammy Carter Bronson
Nov 2008

Written & Illustrated by
Escrito y Ilustrado por Tammy Carter Bronson

Translated by/Traducido por Annou J. Davi

Bookaroos® Publishing, Inc.

Bookaroos® Publishing, Inc.
P. O. Box 8518
Fayetteville, AR 72703 USA
www.bookaroos.com
books@bookaroos.com

Bookaroos® is a registered trademark of
Bookaroos® Publishing, Inc.
All rights reserved.

First Printing, 2004
Second Printing, 2005
Third Printing, 2006
Fourth Printing, 2007
Printed in the United States of America.

Publisher's Cataloging-In-Publication
(Provided by Quality Books, Inc.)

Bronson, Tammy Carter.
    Polliwog / written and illustrated by
Tammy Carter Bronson ; translated by
Annou J. Davi.
    p. cm.
    In English and Spanish.
    SUMMARY: Polliwog's transformation
forces her to enter an unknown world
outside the pond where she embraces her
new life as a frog.
    Audience: Ages 3-10.
    LCCN 2002096929
    ISBN 13: 978-0-9678167-4-6 (Library Binding)
    ISBN 13: 978-0-9678167-5-3 (Softcover)

    1. Tadpoles--Juvenile fiction. 2. Frogs--
Development--Juvenile fiction. [1. Tadpoles--
Fiction. 2. Frogs--Fiction. 3. Animals--
Infancy--Fiction.] I. Davi, Annou J. II. Title.

PZ73B762003   [E]
                           QBI33-1096

For those who
embrace new
beginnings.

Para aquellos que
abrazan nuevos
comienzos.

Polliwog and Perch lived in a pond at the edge of the wood. "I love our pond," Polliwog said to Perch.

Perch was old and wise, and she knew it was time to tell her friend what happens to every tadpole.

"Polliwog, one day you will change and leave the pond."

Polliwog laughed. "No, I won't!" She darted away.

Poliwog y Perca vivían en la charca a la orilla del bosque. "Me encanta la charca," dijo Poliwog a Perca.

Perca era vieja y sabia, y sabía que era el momento para explicar a su amiga lo que acontece a cada renacuajo.

"Poliwog, un día vas a cambiar y salir de la charca."

Poliwog se rió. "¡Yo no voy!" Ella se alejó.

Hide-and-seek was Polliwog's favorite game. She hid in the tall eelgrass and waited for Perch to find her.

Al escondido era el juego favorito de Poliwog. Ella se
escondió en las hierbas altas y esperó a Perca para encontrarla.

Sometimes the frogs spoiled their fun.

"Pesky frogs," grumbled Polliwog. "Why won't they leave us alone?"

A veces las ranas consentían esa diversión.

"Ranas molestas," se quejó Poliwog.

"¿Por qué no nos dejan solas?"

One day Polliwog sprouted tiny legs. She did not like her new legs. She went to see Perch.

"What is wrong with me?"

"Nothing," said Perch. "You are changing."

"My gills feel strange."

"Your lungs are growing. Soon you will breathe air and your gills will stop working."

"Where is air?"

"Above the pond."

Un día a Poliwog le crecieron las patas pequeñitas. A ella no le gustaron las patas nuevas. Fue a visitar Perca.

"¿Qué me pasa?"

"Nada," dijo Perca. "Estas cambiando."

"Mis agallas se sienten raras."

"Tus pulmones estan creciendo. Pronto vas a respirar el aire y tus agallas pararán de funcionar."

"¿Donde está el aire?"

"Afuera de la charca."

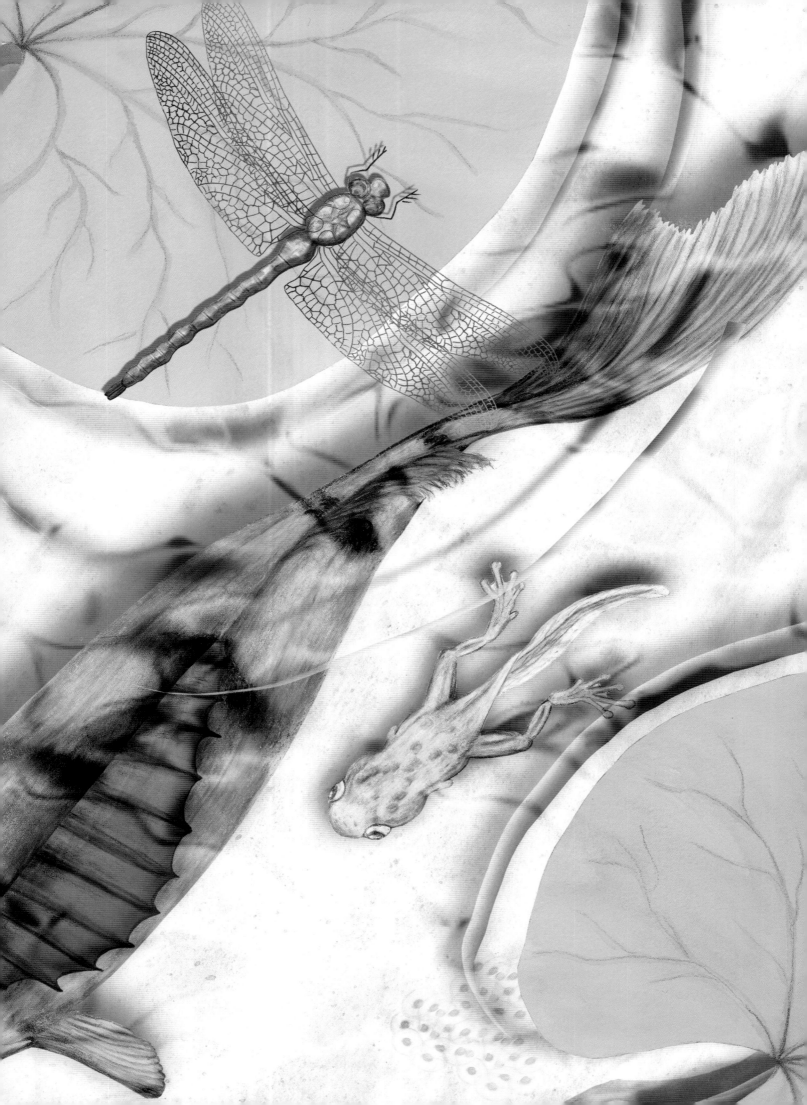

"What is it like outside the pond?"

"I have never been," said Perch.

"I don't want to leave."

"Everything changes, Polliwog. You will have a new life out there. You will see things I cannot see. You will do things I cannot do."

"Like breathe air?"

"Yes."

"Will it hurt to breathe air?"

Perch sighed. She knew a lot of things, but she did not know everything. "I do not know."

"¿Cómo es afuera de la charca?"

"Nunca he ido," dijo Perca.

"Yo no quiero salir."

"Todo cambia, Poliwog. Vas a tener una vida nueva allá. Vas a ver cosas que yo no puedo ver. Vas a hacer cosas que yo no puedo hacer."

"¿Como respirar el aire?"

"Sí."

"¿Me dolerá respirar el aire?"

Perca suspiró. Ella sabía muchas cosas, pero no sabía todo. "Yo no sé."

Finally the day came when Polliwog could barely breathe. Was it already time to go? Polliwog wasn't ready. She hid behind the weeds.

Perch swam over. "Come out, Polliwog. It is time to leave the pond." Polliwog tried to speak but only bubbles came out. "Your voice is already gone. You do not have much time."

Polliwog started to swim away then she looked back at Perch. Perch smiled and said, "Do not be afraid, Polliwog." But Polliwog was afraid. She was afraid of what was beyond the pond, and she was afraid she would never see her friend again.

Por fin llegó el día cuando Poliwog comenzó a respirar. ¿Ya era tiempo de irse? Poliwog no estaba lista. Se ocultó entre los hierbajos.

Perca nadó cerca de ella. "Sal, Poliwog. Ya es tiempo para salir de la charca." Poliwog trató de hablar pero solamente le salían burbujas. "Ya su voz se fue. No tiene mucho tiempo."

Poliwog empezó a nadar y miró hacia atrás a Perca. Perca sonrió y dijo, "No tengas miedo, Poliwog."

Pero Poliwog tenía miedo. Tenía miedo de estar afuera de la charca, y tenía miedo de que nunca iba a ver a su amiga otra vez.

Polliwog climbed toward the surface. Her gills did not work.

Her lungs wanted air. A new world awaited her.

A world with…

Poliwog subió a la superficie. Las agallas no funcionaban.

Los pulmones querían aire. Un nuevo mundo le aguardaba.

Un mundo con…

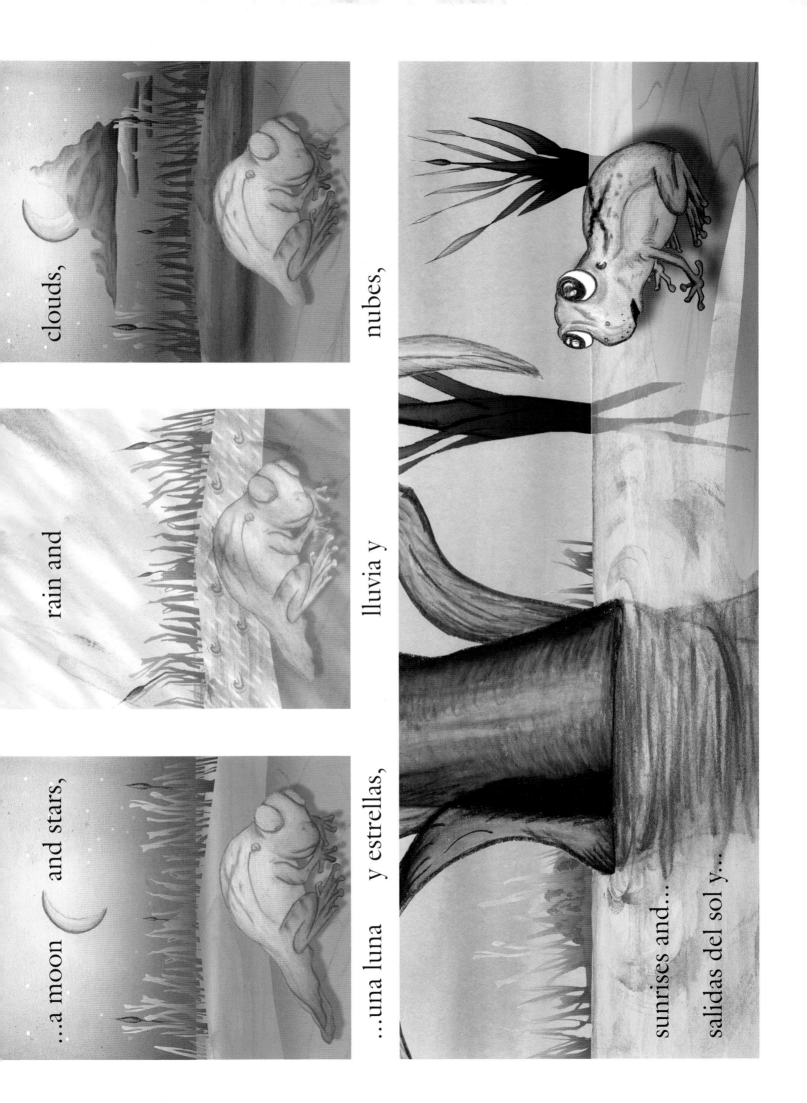

...a moon and stars,

rain and

clouds,

...una luna y estrellas,

lluvia y

nubes,

sunrises and...

salidas del sol y...

...dragonflies.

...libélulas.

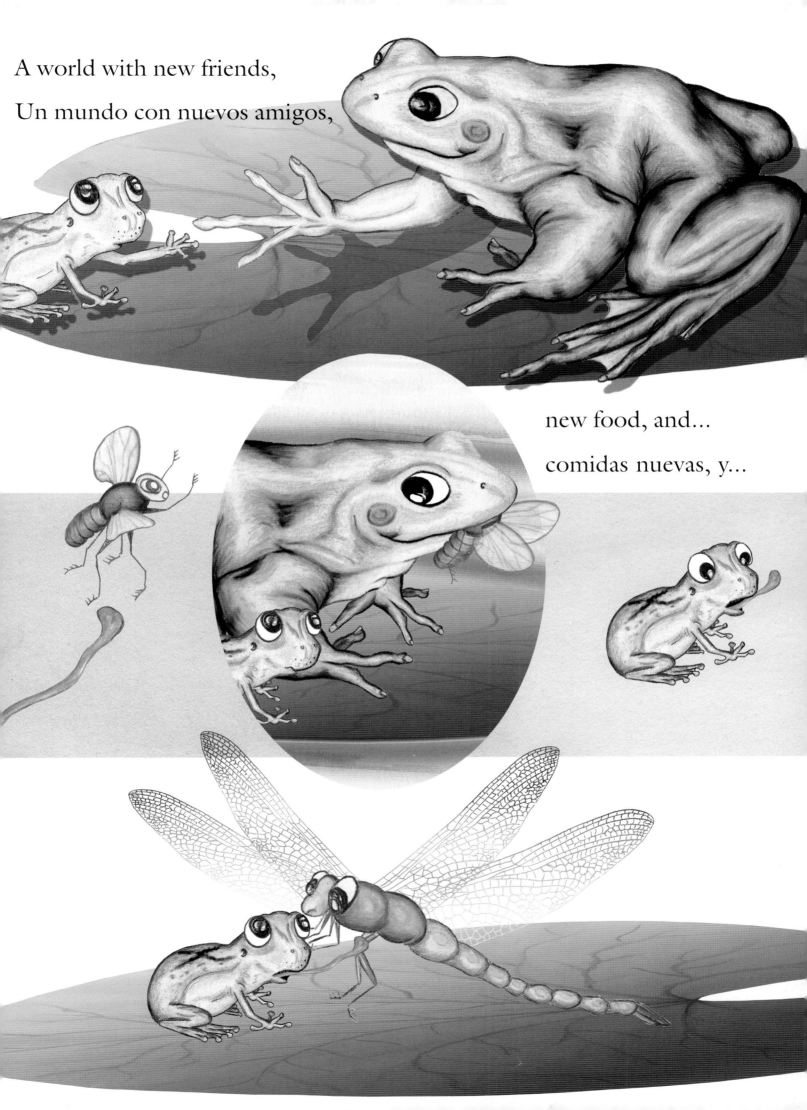

A world with new friends,

Un mundo con nuevos amigos,

new food, and...

comidas nuevas, y...

...new games.

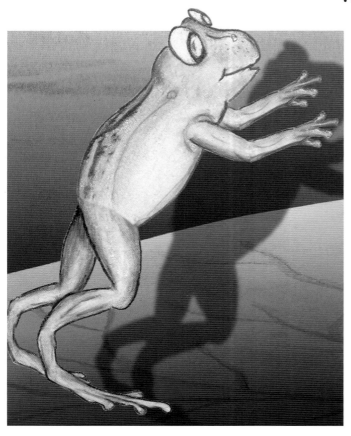

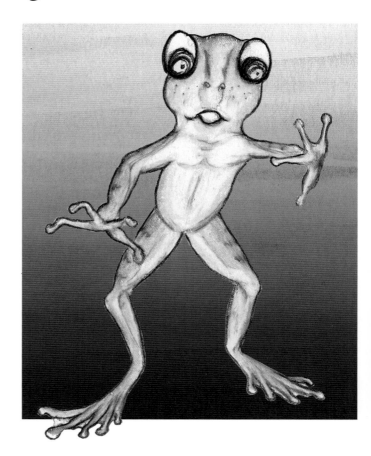

...juegos nuevos.

And when Polliwog saw Perch again...

Y cuando Poliwog volvio a ver a Perca...

...she was a frog.

...ella era toda una rana.

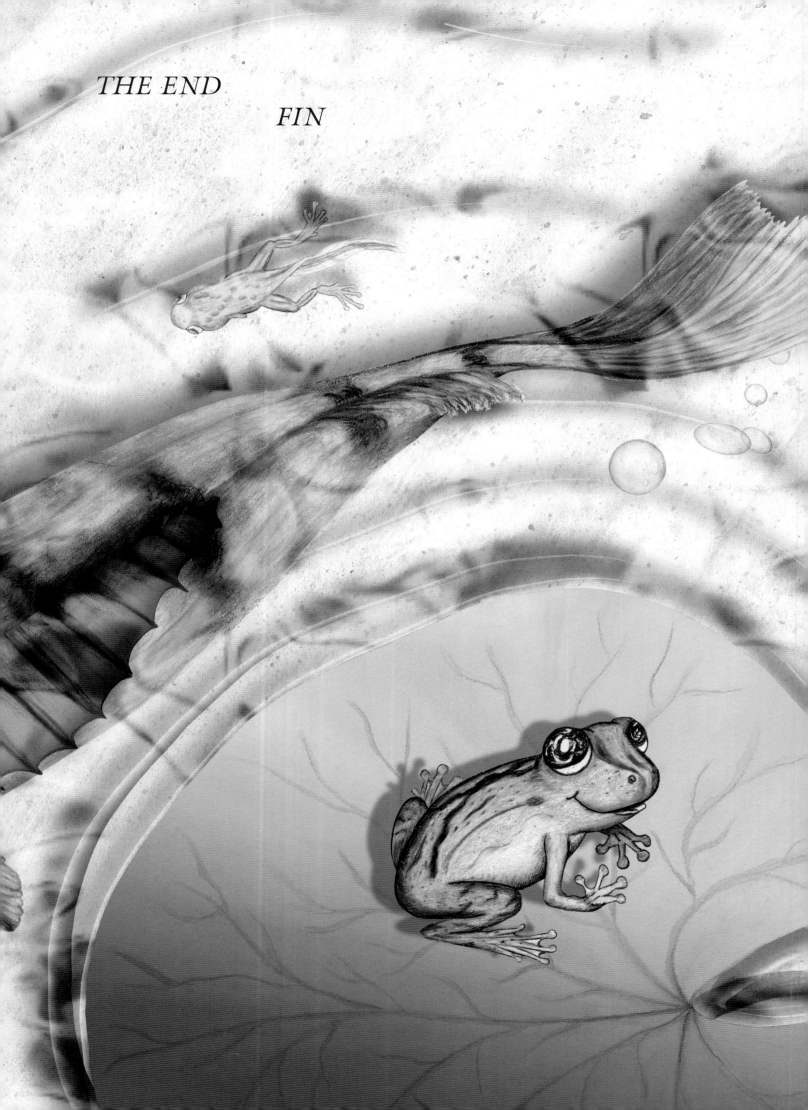

THE END

FIN

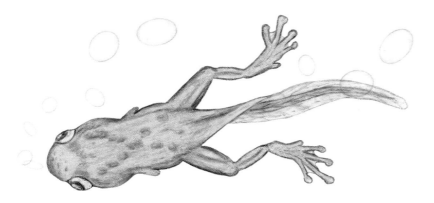

TADPOLES
RENACUAJOS

In the spring a frog lays eggs in fresh, still water. A tiny tadpole emerges from each egg. The tadpole has no legs yet, but it can move by wiggling its tail. A tadpole breathes underwater through gills, and it nibbles on water plants for food. The hind legs appear first. The front legs appear next, and the tail begins to shrink. When the lungs develop, the tadpole can leave the pond and breathe through its nose.

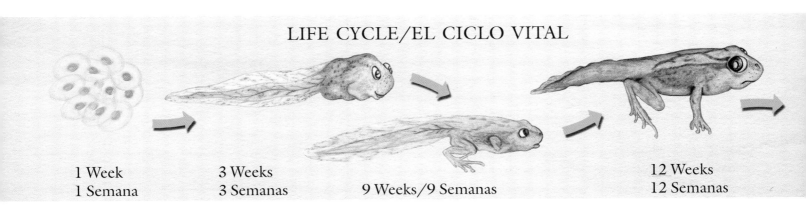

LIFE CYCLE/EL CICLO VITAL

1 Week
1 Semana

3 Weeks
3 Semanas

9 Weeks/9 Semanas

12 Weeks
12 Semanas

En el primavera la rana pone huevos en el agua fresca y tranquila. Un renacuajo diminuto surge de cada huevo. El renacuajo no tiene piernas todavía, pero puede moverse meneando su cola. Un renacuajo respira debajo del agua por agallas, y mordisquea plantas del agua para alimentarse. Las patas traseras aparecen primero. Las patas anteriores aparecen después, y la cola comienza a encogerse. Cuando los pulmones se desarrollan, el renacuajo puede salir de la charca y respirar por su nariz.

FROGS

Frogs are amphibians. Amphibian is a Greek word meaning "double-life" because they live in water and on land. Worldwide there are more than 3,500 species of frogs. The three main types of frogs are true frogs, tree frogs, and toads. When a frog leaves the pond, instead of finding food it will live on nutrients stored in its tadpole tail until it shrinks away. When the tail is gone, the frog hunts for insects and earthworms. Although they have teeth, frogs do not chew their food. They swallow it whole. Frogs drink water by absorbing it through their skin, and in the winter frogs hibernate on land or at the bottom of ponds.

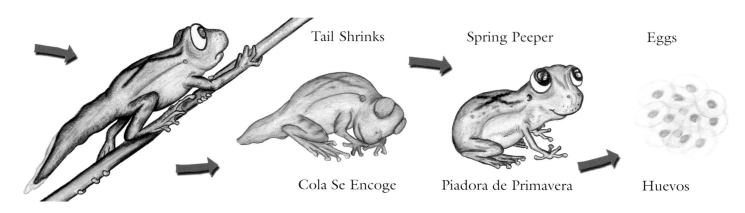

Tail Shrinks   Spring Peeper   Eggs

Cola Se Encoge   Piadora de Primavera   Huevos

Unlike other frogs, toads do not have teeth, their skin is dry and bumpy, and their short, hind legs only allow them to hop small distances.

What kind of frog is Polliwog?

Polliwog has sticky pads on her fingers and toes so she can climb plants. Although she is a tree frog, Polliwog spends most of her time climbing near the ground. The "X" pattern on her back helps identify her as a Spring Peeper. Spring Peepers sing "peep, peep, peep" like a baby chick, but Polliwog will not sing because she is female. Only male frogs sing. Spring Peepers hibernate on land.

Find more frog facts at **www.bookaroos.com.**

RANAS

Las ranas son anfibios. El anfibio es una palabra griega que significa "de vida doble" porque ellos viven en el agua y en la tierra. Mundialmente hay más de 3,500 especie de ranas. Los tres tipos principales de ranas son las ranas verdaderas, las ranas de árbol, y los sapos. Cuándo una rana sale la charca, en vez de buscar alimento vivirá de nutrientes almacenados en su cola de renacuajo hasta que se encoge. Cuándo la cola se va, la rana caza insectos y gusanos. Aunque ellos tengan dientes, las ranas no mastican su alimento. Ellas lo tragan completo. Las ranas beben agua absorbiéndolo por su piel, y en el invierno hibernan en la tierra o en el fondo de charcas.

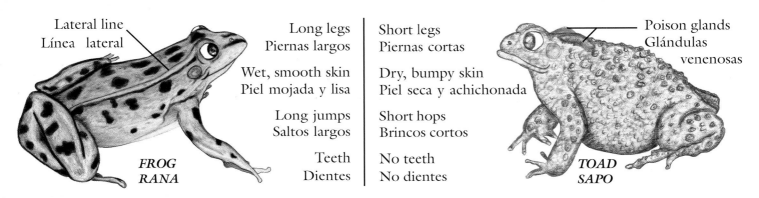

Lateral line
Línea lateral

Long legs
Piernas largos

Wet, smooth skin
Piel mojada y lisa

Long jumps
Saltos largos

Teeth
Dientes

FROG
RANA

Short legs
Piernas cortas

Dry, bumpy skin
Piel seca y achichonada

Short hops
Brincos cortos

No teeth
No dientes

Poison glands
Glándulas venenosas

TOAD
SAPO

A diferencia de otras ranas, los sapos no tienen dientes, la piel es seca y achichonada, y las piernas cortas y traseras sólo permiten que ellos salten pequeñas distancias.

¿Qué clase de la rana es Poliwog?

Poliwog tiene patas pegajosas por lo cual puede subir a las plantas. Por lo tanto ella es una rana de árbol, Poliwog gasta la mayoría de su tiempo subiendo a lugares cerca del suelo. El patrón "X" en su espalda la identifica como una Piadora de Primavera. Las Piadoras de Primavera cantan "pío, pío, pío" como un pollito, pero Poliwog no cantará porque ella es femenina. Las ranas masculinas cantan solamente. Las Piadoras hibernan en la tierra.

*Encuentra los hechos de las ranas más en **www.bookaroos.com**.*

ABOUT THE AUTHOR/ILLUSTRATOR

Tammy Carter Bronson is the author and illustrator of two children's picture books: *Tiny Snail* and *The Kaleidonotes and the Mixed-Up Orchestra*. She lives in Fayetteville, Arkansas with her husband, Shane Bronson. *Polliwog* is her third book.

ACERCA DEL AUTOR/ILUSTRADOR

Tammy Carter Bronson es el autor y el ilustrador de dos libros de niños' ilustrados: *Tiny Snail* y *The Kaleidonotes and the Mixed-Up Orchestra*. Ella vive en Fayetteville, Arkansas con su esposo, Shane Bronson. *Polliwog* es su tercer libro.

To learn more, visit **WWW.BOOKAROOS.COM**.
Aprender más, visita **WWW. BOOKAROOS. COM.**